CHRISTMAS

IS MORE THAN A DAY

By: David Lee Henley

Authors' Note: This is a work of fiction. Names, characters, places, and incidents are a product of the author's imagination. Locales and public names are sometimes used for atmospheric purposes. Any resemblance to actual people, living or dead, or to businesses, companies, events, institutions, or locales is completely coincidental.

Any correspondence with the Author can be made through e-mail at:

brutushenley@hotmail.com

Preface

Unlike all the rest of the year, Christmas has a special place in people's hearts. It is a time to celebrate Christ, a time to be of good cheer, a time to reflect on life and the world, a time to be with family and friends.

A special time to give and receive with love in your hearts, and especially a time to make your children the happiest they can be. To happily watch their eyes light up as they tear into the presents that Santa has brought them.

It is a time to share with the community and the world the unique feelings that only the ethereal Christmas message radiates and conveys to all.

Most anyone you ask could not tell you why they feel this way at this time of year. It is merely a favorite holiday to celebrate, but also, for some reason, it is the most anticipated and observed of any other day of the year.

 It is a magical thing, which somehow exudes excitement, pleasure, and joy in its celebration.

This is a different Christmas story, a real-world Christmas. It is a story of an older man who has lost his belief in how Christmas is supposed to be. A man who has lost that spark that everyone else has for this time of year. A man who just wishes to be left alone in his misery and sorrow.

Introduction

Not everyone can say they had a visit from a spirit. Not everyone would want a visit from a ghost. But some such as Andy would welcome such an appointment if it was from his wife who passed just one year ago. He has never gotten over that loss, and it affects every waking moment.

He lives as if the world had played a cruel joke on him when his wife was taken in death and left him to go on living. The very last thing he would have wanted to do. And to top it all off was the salt on the wound of when it happened; Christmas Eve. How ironic is that? The one time of year that his wife most loved to celebrate. The one time of year, he actually felt like doing for others.

Well, that all changed when Anne passed away. Now he just wallowed in self-pity and sorrow. He was determined to grieve himself to death so that he could once again be with the love of his life.

There was nothing anyone could do to break that stubbornness, not even his children who worried over him.

It was a done deal in his mind, and nothing could shake him out of it. Or so he thought.

This is, after all, Christmas time.

CHRISTMAS

IS MORE THAN A DAY

A SHORT STORY

Opening my eyes, I remember what day it is. I start crying again. I had heard time heals all wounds, but this hurt is beyond repair. Missing Anne is too powerful. This day last year, I awoke to find her lying next to me, cold. I knew she had left me sometime in the night.

The love of my life had departed, and we could never say our goodbyes.

I had such a hard time getting through the following days. Christmas just passed me by, unnoticed. I had no reason to celebrate much less be of good cheer.

I know Anne loved this time of year. She would do all kinds of things, getting ready for the big day, setting up the tree, buying gifts for the children and later the grandchildren, all her friends, and family galore.

It put us in the poorhouse till May when we finally paid off the credit cards.

But I have to say, making her happy was worth it all. I loved seeing the twinkle in her eyes come alive when that time of year came around. It must have rubbed a little off on me too because I liked helping her do all the things she loved.

She made me lug in a big evergreen tree and help her decorate it just right; then, we would sit and take all day wrapping the presents she bought.

It was an unspoken tradition, I suppose, that all the kids and grandkids would come over and unwrap the presents we had so carefully wrapped just before with complete abandon. Ripping and tearing until every last one was seen had been the only objective.

The happy screams of delight coming from the grandkids as the very thing they had asked Santa for magically would be there, and all of them running around in the torn-up paper playing with their toys.

Then, after a while, we would all gather around the table and eat of the food Anne, and the ladies had cooked with love and gaiety. Then we would contentedly sit around and catch up on what we had all been doing that year.

It all seems so distant now; I just don't have the pleasure or joy I used to feel during this time inside me any longer.

A big part of me is missing, and I don't know how to fix it.

I was always good at fixing things. No matter what it was, just let me at it, and before long, it was working again. But not this. Something inside me is broken beyond repair. I am unable to fix myself; too much of me is missing.

I opened the drawer by my bed and re-read the last poem I wrote after Anne's funeral. I used to write her poems all the time, but this one was the last I had left in me. I never touched a pen to write ever again.

It reads:

Yesterday was the hardest day I have ever had to go through.
To pretend I was strong and not lose my sanity.
And now I have to go on and finish this life without you.

With nothing of you to hold on to but our many memories.

Tonight, as I sit in our swing and stare up at the beautiful night sky,
I reminisce of all the times we tried counting the uncountable stars.
I remember how comforting and peaceful it always was and why.
Because in our field of dreams, you were eternally my brightest star.

How do you pick up the pieces of your life and keep on going?
When your world is torn apart because your one love has gone.
To wake up each morning to a home as empty as your soul.
And facing each day with the knowledge, you're all alone.
Darling, I'll miss you as the days begin to lose their light.

And the night commands the hours to slow my thoughts of you.
But someday my time will come and once again we'll be together.
For life has its seasons, but our love endures through it all.

I knew the poem by heart, but it feels better to read it.

I finally got out of bed; it does no good just to lay there. I found it is a lot easier cooking for myself to just make a bowl of cereal. Anne would make me all kinds of things. She loved to cook, and I loved to eat. It was a perfect match.

On the other side of town, Andy's son was having a crisis of his own.

"Linda, I don't know what to do. Dad is so down all the time now, overpowered by grief. Since Mom passed away, he doesn't have that spark of life. I am afraid he is just wasting away; he is grieving himself to death."

Linda said, "Mark, I know this is a trying time. You feel like you need to do something to help your father carry on with life, but this appears to be something he has to work out within himself.

"The best we can do is support him and show that he is not alone. We probably should visit him more often than we have, but to be honest, it is hard on all of us.

"We all cared a great deal for your mother, and it hurts us also not having her around any longer.

"I suppose that is why we don't go over as often as we used to. It reminds us of our losing her. Does that make us culpable in your fathers' anguish? I think so to some extent! But it doesn't change the reality of our feelings.

"Even the kids miss her. She was the anchor that bound all of us together. Without her, we all simply drifted apart. I feel ashamed at even saying it, but without your mother, we have lost the connection as a family unit."

Mark said, "I think I should step up somehow and give assistance and support in helping dad come to grips with his, or I should say, our loss of mother. Life can be very painful at times.

"It is compounded by the season, I am sure. This is the worst time of year to lose a loved one. It always comes to haunt you and spoil the festivities."

"I have been thinking, just mull it over for a while, and we can discuss it later, but as an idea, do you think we could ask Dad to move in with us?"

Linda gasped; "Mark, are you serious? In his condition around the children? Do you think that would be wise?"

Mark said, "please hear me out!

"We bought a home way too big for our needs, and there is ample room for him. I think living alone like he is, is not working out. Here, we could keep an eye on him, and I think all of us together could help everyone in the healing process.

"Besides, he could help with the kids, and he is good at fixing things. We have a lot of things that need attention around here, and we both are pretty busy. Just think about it, will you?

"Not to change the subject but I can't find one person who qualifies for the job of manager for our company. It is strange that in a city this large, not one candidate I have interviewed has passed my necessary requirements. I may have to settle for a person of lesser qualifications, though I am sure that would be a disaster."

Christmas Eve is a time to be happy and thankful, a time to celebrate all your blessings.

Well, that works for most people, but the man next door to Andy does not have much for which to cheer. His company has just decided to downsize due to the economy, and he has been laid off.

This is just great; John was thinking.

The day before Christmas and I get the boot. All those years of dedicated service to the company, and this is what I get? How do I tell my family? What am I going to do now?

As he enters his home, he is greeted by his three children and his wife. They do not know yet of his layoff. He sees no reason to spoil their happiness. There would be plenty of time later for that. He hugs them all and kisses his wife.

She sees in his face, something that should not be there. Yes, something that is there, but should not be, a frown. There should be a smile. He is not smiling.

She asks him, "honey, what's wrong?"

John looks at his wife and not wanting or able to say what happened just yet, said, "let's talk later."

And with that said, he grabbed up his youngest and swung her around all the way to the family room, where he pretended to play with them all happily. He was not going to ruin Christmas for any reason.

As the day waned, everyone was preoccupied and obsessed with their own personal struggles. Each was dealing with their problems as they felt was the only way left to them.

But this is Christmas!

After putting all the kids to bed and having retired to the bedroom, John was finally confronted by his wife, Lisa.

"Ok, John," she demanded. "You have put it off long enough. What is going on?"

Gathering his strength and love for his wife and swallowing his pride, he told her.

He said, "I have been laid off from my job."

Caught off guard with that statement, she said, "oh, John."

Anything else she might have had to say caught in her throat. She didn't know what to say. It was devastating news. All she could think to do was to go to John and hold him in complete silence. Not just to comfort John but also for herself. This could change their whole world.

It was almost midnight, and Andy had finally drifted off to sleep. He never got a lot of sleep anymore. He slept as he could, and that would have to do.

He began a dream, as he often did. Since he obsessed over his wife all the time, is it any wonder he would also dream of her.

She came to him a bit different this time. It was like she was talking to him not as a memory but as one person to another. Like she was right there with him.

 Is this what they call a lucid dream, he wondered. Where it feels so real, and you actually get to interact with it, to control it in some small way. He was pleased about that. To converse with Anne again as if she were still alive.

It started with him waking from his sleep, hearing his name being called.

"Andrew, Andrew, wake up, Andrew; I need to talk to you," said the voice.

Andy knew that voice but was afraid to open his eyes and spoil the dream said, "is that you, Anne? I have missed you so."

Anne said, "Andrew, I need to talk with you and have but a short time."

That got Andy's attention. He sat up in bed and opening his eyes, saw his wife at the foot of the bed. She was translucent and sort of floating in the air. His night light gave off just enough light to make her out.

"Anne, it is you, I am not dreaming, you're really here." He was in ecstasy.

Anne said, "Andrew, I have felt and heard every thought you had toward me. I know I left suddenly, but these things do happen. You don't choose when or how.

"I have come to give your mind rest and peace. To balance your life with reality in this world and to share the knowledge of what is to come. The world, as you know it, is not the end. Life was and will be before and after birth and death.

"So be content in the now of your existence. We will again be together at a later time. This sorrow you have needs to stop. It serves no one and keeps you from living your life to the fullest. There are many who still need you. Don't be selfish in your love.

"Our children have suffered because of your constant grieving. You are tearing their world apart. You need to let me go. Remember me as I remember you, but don't be obsessed with me. Live your life and rejoice in it. Our time will come again."

Andy said, "But Anne, how can I let you go? You were my life, my world."

Anne said, "love your children Andrew, they need you now. I am happy where I am; you need to be content also.

"My time is finished, and I must go. But before I do. There is one thing I must tell you. Find it in your heart to help others less fortunate and in great need. It will reap numerous rewards. I love you. Goodbye, for now, my love."

Anne faded away, leaving Andy alone once again. He stared at the area she had been, frozen in place hoping Anne would return, but eventually, he knew she would not.

He felt such love come over him as he had never felt before. Was she sent back from heaven to give him relief from his despair, to give him closure to his suffering?

His mind was full of thoughts, but then a small light flickering in the window drew his attention. It was faint, but it was growing brighter. He got up and went to the window to see what was causing the light. He saw in an instant.

The neighbors' house was on fire. It was where they had put up the Christmas tree. Somehow, the lights must have started a fire.

He ran to the phone and dialed 911.

"Hello, 911; how may I help you," said the person who answered.

Andy said quickly, "there is a house on fire at 1313 Amar Road. You need to hurry; there are kids in that house." He hung up.

He knew the dispatcher would take too much time, asking a bunch of questions that could wait till later to answer. He needed to make sure everyone was out of the house quickly.

He ran down the stairs dressed only in his pajamas, robe, and moccasins, which he always used as slippers.

Not a minute to waste, he was thinking.

Running out, he saw no one outside the home next door; there was no activity inside the house either.

He started yelling, "hello in there. Wake up. Your house is on fire."

No response.

He ran to the back, where he knew there to be a sliding door into the living room.

He yelled again, "hello in there; your house is on fire, get out."

Still, nothing was coming from inside.

"Ok, he said, I got to get in there quickly."

He looked around and saw a few concrete blocks used to build walls with and grabbed one and threw it into the glass sliding door. That did it. He reached in and unlocked the door. Then moving quickly, he slid it open and ran into the house. It was filled with smoke, and he ducked lower to avoid the heaviest of the smoke. He went into the kitchen and grabbed a towel from the hanger on the oven, and wet it down. He then put that over his nose and mouth so he could better breathe with such choking smoke.

Andy yelled again as he went toward the bedrooms. He finally heard the father yell back through the door. " What is going on? Who are you? What are you doing in my house?"

Andy yelled, "Your house is on fire. You need to get everyone out, now."

John opened his door and seeing the smoke, yelled to his wife, "Lisa, get up, the house is on fire. We need to get the kids out now."

Andy went to the first door and opening it; he saw a little girl in the bed. He ran over and grabbed her, and the covers, and ran outside.

Andy put her down and said, "stay right there, little one." He ran back toward the house as John and Lisa were bringing out the other two children.

He stopped and asked, "where is the main electric box?"

John said, "on the side of the house around the corner going to the back."

Andy ran to it and turned off the electricity.

Coming back, he saw the fire department was arriving. They quickly put out the fire. It was not too bad. They had caught it early. The house would need a lot of repairs, but it was just the area around the tree that did most of the damage.

He stood next to the family, who were devastated. They were out and safe but now had no place to sleep until repairs could be done.

He suddenly remembered Anne's last comment. Help others in need. Did she know this was going to happen? Was this what she was talking about?

He looked at the family. The mother was crying on the husband's shoulder as all the kids were hugging the parents and also crying. It was an unfortunate accident and a terrible thing to witness, and on Christmas eve at that. Tragedy around here is beginning to have a scorecard, Andy thought.

The firemen placed a do not cross tape across the front door and rear broken sliding door. No one could enter the home until the city inspector deemed it safe. That was that.

Ok, Andy boy, what are you going to do. Let them stand there all night. Where is your humanity, man? He felt like a good angel was on one shoulder, and a devil was on the other one fighting it out.

Finally, after arguing with himself for a few minutes, then remembering his wife, and it being Christmas, he spoke softly to the father.

"Look, I have a big house, and it is empty at the moment. I wish that you would share it with me for a while. It is late and tomorrow is Christmas. There is no need for you to stand here all night and freeze.

Please come, be my guests, and we can figure all this out tomorrow."

John was a proud man who would never accept charity for himself, but this was different. He had a family to look after.

He looked at his wife, who he could tell was all for accepting the invitation, and then he looked at his children who were staring at their home. Not a time to be stupid, he said to himself.

He had been standing there and wondering what it was that he did that was so bad as to cause this much trouble to befall him in so short a time. It was devastating and left him a broken man. The only thing that saved him was the thought of his family. He had to carry on for them.

John looked at Andy and said, "I haven't even thanked you for saving us from the fire as yet, and here you are inviting me into your home. I am beyond words, but words must be said.

"First, I wish to thank you for saving my family and myself from the fire. What you did was truly heroic. I can never repay you enough for that alone.

"Now, I must thank you again for caring enough to open your home to us in our time of need.

"Yes, I will take you up on your most generous offer to let us stay with you."

Christmas is a time of heightened emotions, Good and bad. Those having a wonderful time are ecstatic. On the chart of one to ten, they feel eleven. But it also goes that those having troubles during this time have elevated senses of woes that would not reach such a pinnacle during other times of year. It affects everyone the same way.

When morning finally came, Andy called his son and daughter. He explained what had transpired the night before and asked his children to see if they could get some presents and a small tree for the young children of John and Lisa. He would pay them back.

Now, this was totally shocking to Andy's kids. That was the last thing they had expected from their father on Christmas morning. They were surprised and delighted. Not about the situation with the family next door, that was terrible, but how different their father was. He seemed like a changed man, and for the better.

Mark called his friend who happened to own a toy store and told him of the tragedy of

Christmas eve, and his friend asked John to meet him at the store. He came back with the trunk filled with toys for children of the age group Andy had mentioned. Mark and Linda's children had already ripped into their presents, so there was no reason not to go on over and give the children at Dad's house their gifts.

Everyone was still asleep as it had been a long hard night for all of them. Mark and Linda and Andy's daughter and husband, Vicky and Sam, and of course, Andy himself all put up the tree and placed the presents under it just in time for the arrival of the kids and John and Lisa.

John looked at everyone standing around and asked, "what's going on?"

Andy said, "Santa asked me what happened to the children next door, and I told him they were staying here with me.

"Well, he told me, please give the children their presents he had for them, and here they are.

The kids all looked at Andy with big bright eyes, and the oldest one said, "did you say those presents are for us from Santa Claus?"

Andy said, "that's what he told me. They are all yours. Better hurry up and open them before he decides to come back and get them."

That did it. They ran to the pile and like all children, ripped and tore, all while giggling and laughing.

John said, "there you go again. I am never going to be able to pay you back."

John turned away with tears in his eyes and walked into the kitchen, too ashamed to face them any longer.

Andy said, "what did I say, I am sorry. I was just trying to help."

Lisa said, "it is not you; we are so grateful for your kindness. John lost his job yesterday. He had been a manager for years in a big chain of stores, and they just laid him off due to a downsizing in the company.

" He spent years working for them, and they just let him go. So, he is feeling pretty down right now. It has nothing to do with anything you have done.

"He is a proud man and has always been a good provider for us. I guess this being Christmas has made it all the harder to accept."

Mark said, "excuse me for a minute." He went into the kitchen where John had gone.

Linda went to Andy and said, "Mark and I have been discussing your living here all alone, and we think you should come live with us.

"We have a house that just screams of needing someone to take care of it. We are useless in that regard. Also, you could be closer to all of the grandkids and us, of course. It would be a win, win for everyone.

"We also think it would be good way to get the family all back together again. This would be a perfect time for all of us to regain the bond we once had. We all miss that more than you could know."

Andy looked thoughtfully at Linda. She didn't believe, not even for a moment, that he would accept the offer, but she had to try. If today being Christmas didn't get him to change his mind, then it would never happen.

Just then, Mark and John reemerged from the kitchen.

"We have an announcement, John declared. Linda, meet the new Manager for our store.

"I am not giving it to him for any other reason than he is exactly who I have been looking for. Talk about fate intervening. It is a Christmas miracle." John went to Lisa and hugged her.

"Yes, it must be a miracle," John said.

Andy, seeing how well all of the problems worked themselves out, made his own decision.

He began to speak, "Mark, Linda. I accept your invitation to come live with you, on a let's see if it works out contingency. You might live to regret it.

"But then there is always Vicky and Sam over there trying to hide. I might split the time and give everyone some space once in a while.

"As for this house. John, you and Lisa and your kids are welcome to it for as long as it takes to get your own home repaired. No rush.

"I had someone very special come to me recently and told me I needed to be more outgoing and friendly. I plan on doing just that with the time I have left. No more sulking. Life is to be lived."

 Andy stopped for just a moment and looked up to the heavens, then   he said, "Merry Christmas Anne," and then looking at his family and new friends, he said, "and Merry Christmas to all."

BIOGRAPHY

David Henley, born in West Memphis, Arkansas, grew up while moving from place to place. He spent three years in Germany in the Army and has worked many jobs starting at age twelve. Such diversity has allowed a great deal of interaction with society and given him many encounters from which to draw life lessons from in his writings.

In his debut book {POEMS, LYRICS AND DIVERSE THOUGHTS}, he imparts a particular moment in time, that everyone can find within themselves which should awaken a memory they have at one time lived. The lyrics in this book are from the songs he has written.

{THE LAST RIDE IS FREE} is his first thriller fantasy novel about three people and their adventures in the world of criminals and honest society. A journey from the dark side of humanity toward more enlightened soul-searching encounters.

{THE LAST RIDE IS FREE: BOOK TWO} is his continuation of a fantasy thriller novel in a series about the Malone family. It is packed with the same nonstop action as the first book. It has also brought their son into the fold as an agent working alongside his parents, Mario and Julie.

{THE LAST RIDE IS FREE: BOOK THREE} is this finale novel in the series of the Malone Family. It brings the whole family full circle. As usual, it has many adventures and missions but also has secrets about the family that even they were not aware of all finally brought to fruition.

{A DAY IN THE LIFE OF SARGENT SMITH} is a short story about an unknown group of entities searching for what makes a common man different from all others. It is a fantasy action thriller looking into a subject long ignored.

{ALONE, A WAY OF LIFE} is a short story about a man who only wants to be alone, absent from all human contact, but never seems to be able to find that location no matter how far he goes into the wilderness. He is thrust into the middle of a life and death struggle and must keep everyone separated until he can get them all back to the very civilization from which he wants to reject.

Made in the USA
Middletown, DE
31 October 2024

63123241R00021